BASEBALL TALK

GRAND SLAM, FROZEN ROPE, AND MORE BIG-LEAGUE LINGO

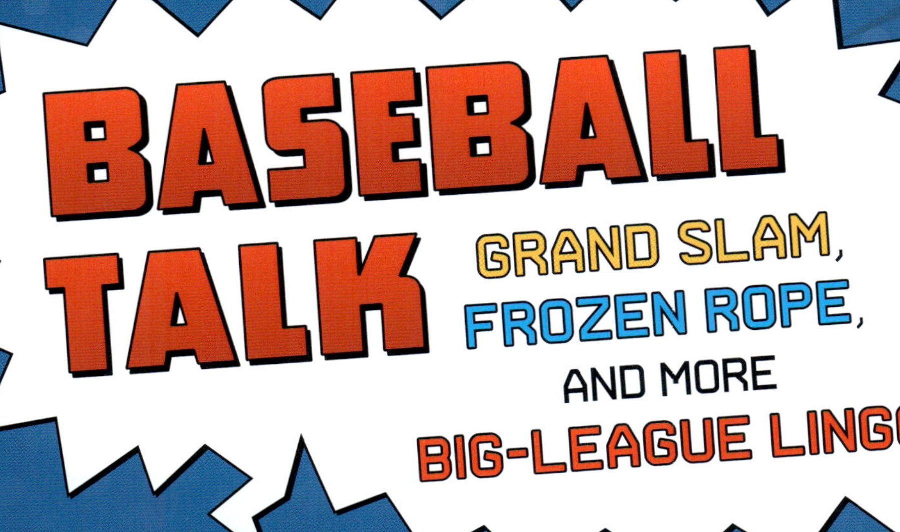

BY MARTIN DRISCOLL

CAPSTONE PRESS
a capstone imprint

Published by Capstone Press, an imprint of Capstone.
1710 Roe Crest Drive
North Mankato, Minnesota 56003
capstonepub.com

Library of Congress Cataloging-in-Publication Data is available on the Library of Congress website.
ISBN: 9781666346985 (hardcover)
ISBN: 9781666347012 (ebook PDF)
Library of Congress Control Number: 2022943651

Summary: Throw a frozen rope! Hit a dinger! Catch a stinger! Discover the meaning of these big-league terms and more in Baseball Talk. Created with Sports Illustrated Kids, this book presents wacky lingo and puzzling phrases from America's favorite pastime.

Editorial Credits:
Editor: Donald Lemke; Designer: Sarah Bennett; Media Researcher: Svetlana Zhurkin; Production Specialist: Katy LaVigne

Image Credits:
Alamy: Cal Sport Media, 12, 24 (bottom), RLFE Pix, 11; Associated Press: 16 (middle), 25 (top), Ashley Landis, 9 (top), Duane Burleson, 29, Greg Trott, 7, Kathy Willens, 26 (bottom); Dreamstime: Jerry Coli, 4; Getty Images: Chicago History Museum, 9 (bottom); Library of Congress: 10 (bottom); Newscom: Icon Sportswire/Carlos Herrera, 21, Icon Sportswire/Daniel Bartel, 27, Icon Sportswire/Nick Wosika, 23; Shutterstock: Andre Adams, 20 (gopher), DoyanDesign (burst background), cover and throughout, ecco, 22, GB_Art, 14 (top), Ginatra Design, 8 (top), Gleb Guralnyk, 26 (top), HitToon, 25 (bottom middle), Ken Benner, 10 (potato), Kong Vector, 13, Leonid studio, cover (baseball), cover and throughout (mike), cover and throughout (dotted background), lineartestpilot, 28 (banjo), Mochipet (baseball), 20, 24, 26, Now Design, 24 (top), Photo Works, 19, PianoMark, 15 (top), Ron Leishman, 6 (top), Ron Leishman, 28 (baseball player), Samuray Studio, 25 (bottom right), Sopelkin, 25 (bottom left), Svetlana777, 8 (bottom), Tanya Sid, 6 (bottom), Tony Oshlick, 16 (top), Tribalium, 18, Vector Tradition, 10 (fly), VudiArts, 15 (bull); Sports Illustrated: Erick W. Rasco, 5, 14 (bottom), John W. McDonough, 17

All records and statistics in this book are current through the 2021 season.

Table of Contents

WE'RE TALKING BASEBALL

Baseball fans love the sights and sounds of the game. They love to see big swings, towering hits, and leaping catches. They love to hear the crack of the bat and the roar of the crowd.

Baseball fans also love to *talk* about the game! They talk between pitches as each game goes on. They talk between games all season long. And they talk between seasons all through the winter months.

FACT Major League Baseball (MLB) includes the National League and the American League. The National League formed in 1876. Then the American League formed in 1900. The champions of each league faced each other in the first World Series in 1903.

Major League Baseball has a history that stretches back more than 120 years. That's just pro baseball as fans know it today. People have been playing, watching, and talking about the game since the mid-1800s.

During those years, baseball created a language of its own. This language can be funny and surprising. It can also be odd and puzzling. The language of baseball is yet another thing fans love about the game.

Mookie Betts batted leadoff for the Boston Red Sox during the 2018 American League Division Series against the New York Yankees.

CHAPTER ONE

BATTER UP

leadoff hitter ▶ the player listed first in the team's batting order

cleanup hitter ▶ fourth in the batting order, usually the team's best hitter

lumber ▶ a wooden baseball bat

The action in any baseball game begins with the **leadoff hitter**. He or she is first to bat for their team. Their job is to get on base in any way they can. The leadoff hitter might get a walk. They might slap a single just over the infielders' heads. They might smack a line drive to the outfield gap for a double.

FACT The batters who are "on deck" and "in the hole" follow the current hitter. The on-deck batter goes next. Then comes the batter in the hole. The terms came from the world of sailors and ships.

Leadoff hitters come in many shapes and sizes. Some are slim and speedy. Some are strong and slow. A good leadoff hitter is someone who gets on base often. That's what matters most. Why? If they get on base, the team's best hitters can drive them home.

Rickey Henderson batted leadoff for many MLB teams, including the Oakland Athletics. During his Hall-of-Fame career (1979–2003), he stole a record 1,406 bases with his lightning-quick speed.

Each team's batting order includes nine hitters. The best hitter in the lineup usually bats fourth. They are called the **cleanup hitter**. The cleanup must be good with the **lumber**. Their job is to clear the bases with a home run or another long hit. That's where the name comes from. If they do their job perfectly, the player cleans up the bases.

Baseball fans know Shohei Ohtani hits a lot of home runs. The Los Angeles Angels superstar is one of the best power hitters in the game. Ohtani also hits a lot of **frozen ropes**. A frozen rope is a hard-hit ball that travels in a straight line.

In 2021, Ohtani smacked a double that left his bat at 119 miles (192 kilometers) per hour. The ball did not fly very high. But it kept on going. And going. It finally landed near the outfield wall. No MLB batter hit a ball harder that season.

FACT A low and hard throw by a fielder can also be called a frozen rope.

Los Angeles Angels star Shohei Ohtani hits a home run against the Baltimore Orioles in 2021.

A **Texas leaguer** is the opposite of a frozen rope. A Texas leaguer is soft fly ball that goes over the infielders and lands in front of the outfielders.

The term goes back to a player named Ollie Pickering. Pickering was a star in the Texas League. In 1901, he moved up to the Cleveland Blues in the American League. He had hits in his first seven at-bats. All of them were short **fly balls** that landed for singles. His teammates nicknamed such hits Texas leaguers.

Ollie Pickering, 1903

A home run is sweet by any name, and baseball players have many names for home runs. Babe Ruth hit lots of home runs. He also hit lots of **dingers**, **taters**, **bombs**, **four-baggers**, and, **big flies**. He even hit quite a few **grand slams**.

Before the Babe came along, Ned Williamson of the Chicago White Stockings had the record for home runs in a season. He hit 27 homers in 1884.

Ruth broke that record with 29 dingers in 1919. He smashed his own record the next year with 54. In 1927, Ruth hit 60 home runs. That number stood as the record for more than 30 years.

Babe Ruth, early 1920s

Wally Moon couldn't hit like Ruth. Still, he made a name for himself as a power hitter. Moon played for the Dodgers soon after the team moved to Los Angeles. While Dodger Stadium was being built, the team played in the L.A. Coliseum. The Coliseum wasn't made for baseball. The left field wall was just 250 feet from home plate. Moon had a knack for hitting fly balls that soared high into the air. Some of those high flies became short home runs in the Coliseum. They were nicknamed **moon shots**.

Today, a home run that soars high *and* far is called a moon shot.

Wally Moon inside L.A. Memorial Coliseum, where he hit many moon shots during his career as a Los Angeles Dodger

Home runs are thrilling, but sometimes a batter can do better. On a truly great day, a player might hit for **the cycle**. That means they hit a single, double, triple, and home run in the same game.

Hitting for the cycle is a rare feat in the major leagues. It happened only 313 times from 1876 to 2016. Few players have done it more than once in their career. Only five have done it three times. A natural cycle is even rarer. That's when the hitter gets a single, double, triple, and home run in that order.

Former Texas Rangers All-Star Adrián Beltré hit for the cycle three times during his major league career.

Most batters would rather hit a **walk-off** than a homer—or even a cycle. A walk-off is a hit that brings in a run and ends the game. It can happen only in the bottom half of the last inning. A walk-off means the home team wins.

Oakland A's pitcher Dennis Eckersley came up with the phrase in the 1980s. He used it when a home run wins the game. In that case, the losing pitcher has a lonely walk off the field. Today, a walk-off is any hit that brings in a game-ending run.

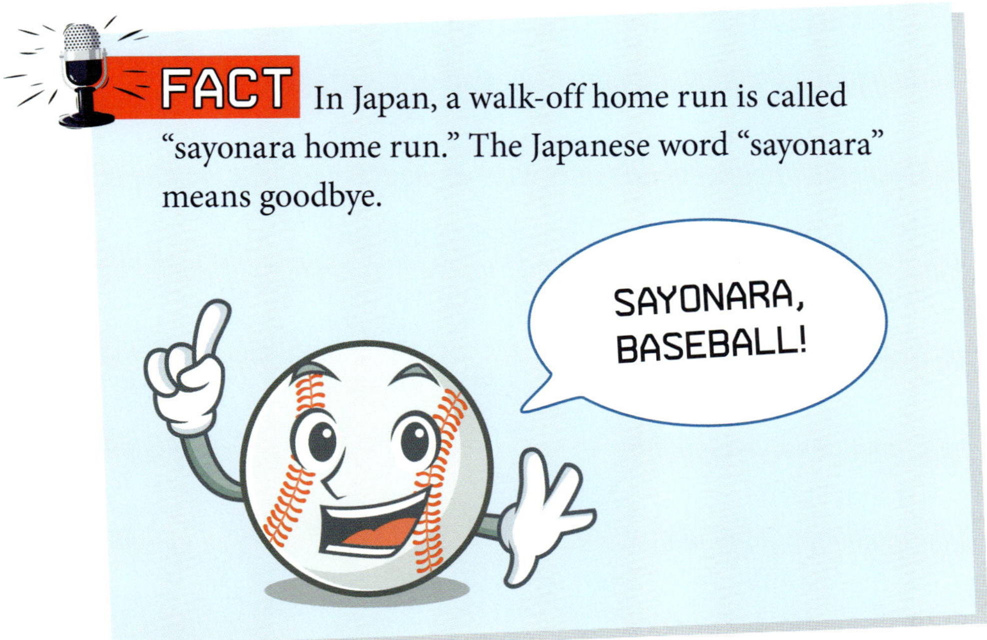

FACT In Japan, a walk-off home run is called "sayonara home run." The Japanese word "sayonara" means goodbye.

CHAPTER TWO

ON THE MOUND

ace ▶ a team's best starting pitcher

the hill ▶ the pitcher's mound

bullpen ▶ the area where relief pitchers warm up

When a team sends its **ace** to **the hill**, their opponents take notice. A team's ace is its best starting pitcher. Most teams have a five-man rotation of starters. That means every five games the ace gets the start.

Not so long ago, an ace was expected to pitch seven, eight, or nine innings. That has changed. Today, managers usually call for help from the **bullpen** earlier in the game.

All-Star starter Max Scherzer pitches for the Washington Nationals in 2017.

Players warm up in the bullpen at Constellation Field in Sugar Land, Texas.

The bullpen is where relief pitchers warm up. It is an enclosed area beside the field. Often the bullpen is located beyond the outfield wall. Followers of baseball history disagree about where the term came from. Some say the name comes from the world of rodeos. At a rodeo, bulls are held in small pens before being released into the ring.

FACT A "closer" is a pitcher who specializes in finishing games. He usually has to get only the last few outs. But the pressure is high when the game is close.

Nolan Ryan was once the most feared pitcher in baseball. Ryan played for four MLB teams over 27 years. He was a lean but powerful right-hander. He could bring the **heat**. He could throw **smoke**. Ryan could bring the **gas**. He struck out more batters than anyone in history. And if a batter crowded the plate, Ryan might throw some **high cheese**.

Nolan Ryan, 1974

FACT "Chin music" is another name for a pitch that goes near a batter's head. Sometimes pitchers throw chin music or high cheese on purpose. They want to warn the batter about standing too close to the plate.

During a 1974 game, Ryan fired a fastball that reached 100.9 mph (162 kph). Officials used a radar gun to measure the pitch speed. Ryan was the first pitcher ever shown to have topped 100 mph.

Imagine having that fastball zip past your ear. Then imagine stepping back into the batter's box to await Ryan's next pitch.

FACT Aroldis Chapman now has the record for the fastest pitch in MLB history. In 2010, the lefty threw a fastball that hit 105.1 miles (169 km) per hour.

Aroldis Chapman, 2010

junk ▸ a slow pitch that has lots of movement

off-speed pitch ▸ any pitch slower than a fastball

breaking ball ▸ a pitch that curves

bender ▸ another name for a curveball

curveball ▸ a pitch thrown with spin that makes it drop and move to the side as it nears home plate

changeup ▸ a slow pitch thrown with the same motion as a fastball

Not every big-league pitcher has a cannon for an arm. Some pitchers make a living by throwing a lot of **junk**. Some of them can't throw fastballs at scary speeds. They rely on **off-speed pitches** and **breaking balls**.

Clayton Kershaw used a big **bender** to become a superstar. The Dodgers pitcher is famous for his **curveball**. Kershaw is left-handed, so his bender moves down and to the right. Often it crosses the plate going less than 75 mph (121 kph). But that doesn't help batters much. Kershaw has led the National League in strikeouts three times. He was an All-Star eight times between 2011 and 2021.

Three-time Cy Young Award winner Clayton Kershaw pitches for the Los Angeles Dodgers in 2010.

Kyle Hendricks of the Chicago Cubs throws one of the best **changeups** in MLB today. A changeup looks just like a fastball when it leaves the pitcher's hand. But it travels slo-o-o-wly to the plate. Batters swing too soon and end up looking silly. Hendricks' fastball is nothing special. It comes in below 90 mph (145 kph), but he fools batters with his off-speed stuff. In 2021, Hendricks led National League pitchers in wins.

FACT Jamie Moyer seemed to get better with age. The lefty pitched for eight teams over 25 seasons. He was known for off-speed pitches and pinpoint control. He won 16 games when he was 45 years old. He last pitched in MLB at age 49.

When a curveball doesn't curve, it becomes a **meatball**. The same is true when a fastball isn't very fast. A meatball is any pitch that is easy to hit. That's different from a **gopher ball**, which is a pitch hit for a home run.

Bert Blyleven is in the Hall of Fame, and he was famous for his curveball. But for one year, he was the king of the gopher ball. In 1986, Blyleven was pitching for the Minnesota Twins, one of the five MLB teams he played for. He had a good season. He won 17 games even though the Twins had a losing record. But Blyleven also set the MLB record for home runs allowed in a season. Blyleven pitched in 36 games that season. He gave up 50 home runs. He also proved that even a top pitcher can throw a lot of gopher balls.

Former San Diego Padres player Yangervis Solarte gets hit by a pitch in the game against the Arizona Diamondbacks in 2016.

Batters love to see a meatball coming their way. They are not so fond of **beanballs**. A beanball is a pitch thrown at a batter. Some people say it's a beanball only if it is thrown at the batter's head. Some say it's a beanball only if it actually hits the batter. Others still call it a beanball even if the batter dives out of the way.

FACT Jamie Moyer threw great junk, but he also served up lots of gopher balls. Moyer gave up 522 home runs during his long MLB career. That's more than any other pitcher in history.

CHAPTER THREE

IN THE FIELD

The Show ▶ the major leagues

Gold Glove ▶ an award given to the best fielder at each position

leather ▶ baseball glove

Francisco Lindor might be the best fielding shortstop in MLB. He came to **The Show** with Cleveland in 2015. Since then he has won a pair of **Gold Glove** Awards. He has also been an All-Star four times. Lindor joined the New York Mets in 2021. Fans call him "Mr. Smile" and know him for his skill with the **leather**.

Many fans probably don't know why his position is called shortstop. Other fielding positions have names that are simple. The first baseman plays near first base. The center fielder covers center field. Everyone gets the idea. But where does "shortstop" come from?

The name goes back to the early days of the game. One baseball club began putting a player in the "short field." His main job was to get the ball from the outfield to the infield quickly. Other teams soon did the same thing.

In time, the position moved closer to the batter. The name changed over time too. The shortstop joined the third baseman on the left side of the infield.

Francisco Lindor plays shortstop in the major leagues.

23

worm burner ▶ a hard ground ball

hot corner ▶ third base

bag ▶ a base

cannon ▶ a strong throwing arm

Commissioner's Trophy ▶ the trophy presented to the team that wins the World Series

If a batter hits a **worm burner** to the **hot corner**, it's time for the third baseman to shine. Third basemen often line up even with the **bag**. Sometimes they move closer still to the infield grass. Lots of hard-hit balls come their way. You might even say balls come in hot. A good third baseman must be quick with his glove. It helps if he also has a **cannon**. Those long throws across the infield aren't easy.

FACT Nolan Arenado might be today's best fielder at third base. He won eight Gold Gloves while playing for the Colorado Rockies. Before the 2021 season, the Rockies traded him to the St. Louis Cardinals.

Hall of Fame player Brooks Robinson fields a
ground ball during the 1971 All-Star Game.

In MLB history, Brooks Robinson stands out
among third basemen. Robinson played for the
Baltimore Orioles. He was an All-Star 18 times. He
helped his team capture the **Commissioner's Trophy**
twice. Robinson also won 16 Gold Glove Awards.
From 1960 to 1975, Robinson took that prize in the
American League every year. His record will be tough
for another third baseman to top.

Kevin Kiermaier and Byron Buxton play center field like daredevils. Kiermaier has been a Gold Glove winner for the Tampa Bay Rays. Buxton has won a Gold Glove for the Minnesota Twins. Both players have great speed and cover a lot of ground. Both of them also have strong arms. Both often make plays that seem impossible. Highlight reels are full of their **circus catches**.

Tampa Bay Rays center fielder Kevin Kiermaier makes a diving catch.

Minnesota Twins center fielder Byron Buxton crashes into the outfield wall after making a catch against the Chicago White Sox.

Unfortunately, they have another thing in common. Kiermaier and Buxton get hurt a lot. They miss a lot of games due to injuries. But when they are healthy, they play only one way. You will see them **laying out** to catch hard-hit balls. You will see them charging in to make **shoestring catches**. And you will see them crashing against outfield walls as they rob hitters of home runs.

FACT Outfielder Mookie Betts is a star for the Dodgers. He is called a "five-tool" player. That means he can run, throw, and field well. He can also hit for power and for a high batting average.

CHAPTER FOUR

THE OLD BALLGAME

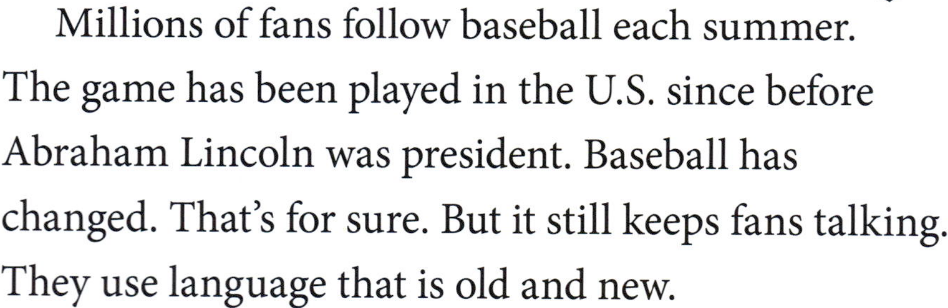

Millions of fans follow baseball each summer. The game has been played in the U.S. since before Abraham Lincoln was president. Baseball has changed. That's for sure. But it still keeps fans talking. They use language that is old and new.

A fan might dismiss a batter as a **banjo hitter**. That means he doesn't hit with power. The term has been around for about 100 years. A player named Snooks Dowd came up with it. He thought a soft hit sounded like a banjo being plucked. Dowd spent most of his playing years in the **bush leagues**. He played in only 16 games in the majors. But he lives on in baseball talk.

The language of baseball is always changing.
Thirty years ago, a walk-off meant one thing. It was
a game-ending home run. Now a walk-off can be any
hit that brings in a run to end the game.

In 2021, the Detroit Tigers were facing the
Houston Astros. The game was tied in the bottom of
the tenth. With a runner on third, the Tigers tried a
squeeze play. Robbie Grossman dropped down a bunt.
The runner beat the throw to home. Game over. The
Tigers celebrated the walk-off bunt as if it had been a
moon shot.

Members of the Detroit Tigers celebrate their win over the Houston Astros in June 2021.

Glossary

highlight (HYE-lite)—the best or most interesting part
of something

knack (NAK)—an ability to do something difficult or tricky

position (puh-ZISH-uhn)—the place where someone or
something is, such as on a baseball diamond

radar gun (RAY-dar GUHN)—a device used to check the
speed of a moving object, like a baseball or a vehicle

rotation (ruh-TAY-shuhn)—a system in which turns are taken
in a particular order

Read More

Buckley, James Jr. *It's a Numbers Game! Baseball: The Math Behind the Perfect Pitch, the Game-Winning Grand Slam, and So Much More!* Washington, DC: National Geographic Kids, 2021.

Chandler, Matt. *Baseball's Greatest Walk-Offs and Other Crunch-Time Heroics.* North Mankato, MN: Capstone, 2021.

Pryor, Shawn. *Baseball's Craziest Catches!* North Mankato, MN: Capstone, 2021.

Internet Sites

Baseball: A Timeline
pbs.org/kenburns/baseball/timeline

MLB Kids
mlb.com/fans/kids

National Baseball Hall of Fame: Our Stories
baseballhall.org/our-stories

Index

About the Author

Martin Driscoll is a former newspaper reporter and longtime editor of children's books. He is also the author of several sports books for children, including biographies of legendary stars of boxing, baseball, and basketball. Driscoll lives in southern Minnesota with his wife and two children.